PROLOGUE

T he sun beats down relentlessly as the toga-clad soldiers drag the seemingly lifeless body of a young man across the camp to a barren hillside. The young man, his body already scarred from many beatings raises his head at the view up ahead, seeing the bodies of 3 others, crucified and left to hang from the rudimentary crosses erected in the harsh, arid environment he once called home.
The soldiers mutter to one another with snatched phrases heard by the young man; "supernatural. Not of this world. Evil"

They hoist the young man into place on the cross, the rope biting at his skin. He opens his mouth to scream out but blackness engulfs him, striking him deaf and mute, until he hears voices talking in low, urgent tones.

He opens his eyes as a man wearing a white smock pulls an oxygen mask over his face and reappears a second later holding a huge hypodermic needle. He fights again, finding the restraints smoother now, leather and not as abrasive as the hemp rope. He hears machinery and electronic beeps. An intercom. A gurney; its wheels whispering on linoleum flooring.

A scream- which he recognises as his own- pierces the air. Recycled, sterile air. He opens his mouth, gasping. Sucking as much into his lungs as possible, ready for another, even louder scream, before a crash of thunder booms across the room as he tries to sit up and pull at the restraints which are now simply cotton bedsheets. He thrashes and rips them off before lying down on his sodden, sweat-soaked bed, breathing heavily to drown out the panic rising in his gut.

CHAPTER 1

I am 12.

That's what I am.

12?

12 what?

People? No! Obviously.

Eyes? Nope.

Toes? No! I'm not a fucking Witches' cat!

12 years old.

Well, I look 12, but I don't actually know how old I am.

I know the fastest way to kill, maim, incapacitate and neutralise with my bare hands. I know how to strip an array of firearms from the tiniest pistol to the biggest rifle or machine gun. I know how to drive a car, a lorry, a tank and a bus. I can sail a ship or fly an aircraft. I know how to fire a bow, use a knife, and swing an axe.

I know how much pressure it takes to break bones. I know what arterial blood looks like. I know what colour a human heart is and how many times it pumps in my hand before it ceases to function. I know what entrails - human and animal look like, and I know what I look like: I look like a 12 year old boy. Slightly built with a smattering of pre-pubescent spots here and there, cold blue eyes, and hair that never seems to grow. I know I've got a fucking touch of Tourette's too. Oh... and a wicked sense of humour.

I also know there is something 'wrong' with me.

How do I know?

Well, put it this way; I've looked 12 years old since before I can remember: Since I stormed the beaches of Normandy in 1944. Since the rebellion of 1837. Since The Wars of the three kingdoms from 1639. Since that big scrap at Hastings in 1066.

Wars I have played my part in. So many wars. So much pain and suffering. So much..... So much.... experience!

So many skills acquired and honed and practiced and pressure tested. So many reasons for who and what I am now. Which is what?

A killer. I'm a kucking filler!

An assassin sounds too glamorous, a warrior sounds noble, and a knight sounds chivalrous.

So, no, I'm just a killer. Plain and simple.

A 12 year old 'thing' that has spent centuries fighting and killing.

Years spent living and training with Vikings, Romans, Monks, Mongols, tribes and armies.

A lifetime of forgotten empires, of foreign lands, of punishment, of reward, of laughter, of sadness. A road well-travelled.

Anyway, introductions over, you're probably bored now, so I'll tell you WHERE I am: I'm high. Very high. Not in the psychological sense. I'm physically high, as in up high.

I'm in my 'apartment' according to the Man-bun-having estate-fucking-agent! But it's actually a fucking flat with a vista that stretches for miles. I'm waiting for my orders from the agency I work for. The agency that pays me for the work I do, which in turn pays for this 'apartment' I own.

I am 12. Not agent 12, not number 12, not boy 12.

Just 12. The most dangerous man/boy/thing on the fucking planet, and I mean THE most dangerous on the planet.

CHAPTER 2

I sit in my darkened room in stasis. Waiting patiently, almost in a meditative state.

Waiting for a sign, a sign from the Gods, the Email Gods.

Shut the fuck up now 12. You're rambling like an old fart!

I'm actually waiting for an alert tone to tell me I've got an alert on the hi-tech communications device I use to alert my handler that I'm alert.

In other words, Addy, who is my handler, writes an email, saves it to the draft folder, alerts me to that fact and gives me a chance to read it before I delete it and reply in the same way.

Easy! No messages actually sent, so no trail to pick up on, no snooping, no spying, and no proof. Perfect deniability, which is what I do, which is why I get paid the big bucks!

Pounds 12! It's fucking pounds, fucking shillings, and fucking pence!

ALL OK? GOOD HOLIDAY? ENJOY BEING THE EPITOME OF SARTORIAL ELEGANCE WHILST IT LASTS OLD BOY! GOOD LUCK, SAFE JOURNEY AND GODSPEED!!

Addy is a bit eccentric, a bit of a wordsmith. Simple, plain English would have sufficed. I know what I'm doing, I'm not a fucking kid!

Well... er, technically I suppose I am. Or am I?

Anyway. Enough of this soliloquy (see, I can wordsmith too), I've got fucking work to do.

CHAPTER 3

The shelter was full for the night owing to the shit weather and the epidemic that is homelessness.

Men, women, children, and the perfunctory dog all trying to upgrade from sleeping bag and shopfront to sleeping bag and roll mat.

Bodies lying haphazardly in direct contravention of health and safety law... Yeah, right! It's ok for us to sleep rough though eh? Fucking Government piss me right off!

So here I am, lying in front of an old Maplin store with a sleeping bag, a couple of towels, and a cardboard box, and despite my healthy bank balance all I have for sustenance is a bottle of Lucozade and some chips (not fucking fries!) courtesy of the sweet lady who saw me from the queue in the chippy and 'paid it forward'.

It's now day three of the job and still nobody has tried to recruit me or the other kids on the street.

I've been shouted at, threatened, and moved on more times than I can remember. I even had to spark some fucking dick out who thought he'd have a piss over me for a laugh! But it's all about appearances now, appearances and the job at hand so I've attached myself to another group of homeless lads who keep saying "y'ight Bruv?" "Safe Bro?" and talking about the 'Po-Po, Feds, Mandem, and Tings! - Fucking imbeciles!

I think they can gauge my uncertainty and gullibility, after all, my cover story has been kept simple: middle class, only child, Dad dead, Mum's new fella a prick, bunking school, running away from home to the bright lights of the big city to make some money and 'show them all!'.

It's dark now as we settle for the night with the local hard men wandering past shouting at us to "get a fucking job" and reminding us we've "always got money for cider!" blissfully unaware that I actually have got a job and could snap their necks like matchsticks if I wanted to!

Note to self: I fucking hate piss-heads!

Most of my 'Bredrin' are asleep or intoxicated now so I'm hyper-alert, managing to get by with only 30 mins of sleep a day quite comfortably and keeping a watchful eye for anything. Something. Somebody to come and 'snatch' me.

Turns out we don't have to wait long as I'm aware of some 'lads' staring at us intently and nodding subtly to one another.

"Wanna make some dough?" One lad shouts.

He's thickset, with a Mike Tyson face tattoo, wearing Lacoste trainers and a Fred Perry polo shirt with a thick gold bracelet and matching necklace - fucking prick!

"Yo! Wanna make some dough?" He repeats.

"Get yourselves a bit of food and a room for the night"

One of our group, Joey shouts "Nah Bruv, we doin' ok innit?"

"Wasn't talkin' to you Joey!" Tattoo retorts "so wind ya fuckin' neck in!"

"You lads? You!? Oi, Bieber!" he continues without taking a breath and nodding at me.

"Me? Er, doing what exactly please?" I ask.

"Doing what exactly please!!?" He mimics whilst talking in a posh voice.

"Fuck me, you're a bit green ain't ya? Fresh meat lads!"

"Don't really matter does it!?" He intones threateningly. "A ton. Easy fucking money. Specially for a posh little twat like you Bieber!"

I swallow hard, playing the role of the 'fresh meat' perfectly "er, no. Thank you. I'll leave it I think".

"Not asking, fuckin' tellin! Come on Bieber, I'll make you a rich kid again!"

Hands grab me. I try and resist weakly as I'm propelled out into the high street and told to "keep fuckin' walking".

Up ahead is a white Audi estate, my trained eyes take it all in; registration, model, the trolley dink on the rear door, the two tiny aerials, the blacked-out windows, the lights hidden behind the front grill, and the two obvious undercover Policemen staring with thinly-veiled disgust at me, tattoo and his mates.

The driver buzzes his window down and speaks to tattoo "new recruit?"

"Er yeah, fucking public schoolboy, soft as shite!"

He looks from me to tattoo. "Been to many public schools have you?"

Tattoo bristles and opens his mouth to reply then thinks better of it and just shakes his head.

"Put him in the back then if you will"

And that's it. In full view of the homeless population I'm dumped in the back of an undercover Police car by Tattoo and co.

The window buzzes back up, the engine starts, the locks clump down, and we're off.

"You're not going to be a pain in the arse are you son?" The passenger asks.

"Er... no. Not at all. Am I in trouble?" I reply with a hint of fear in my voice.

"You'll be fine, just do as you're told, when you're told and there'll be nothing to worry about" he smiles, pulling a pillowcase over my head.

The driver turns the radio up to drown out their conversation as I catch the debate of the pros and cons involved with plasti-cuffing me:

"Looks bad, what if they damage his wrists before we hand him over?"

"Yeah, but what if he escapes?"

"Nah, he's about 8 stone soaking wet!" and so it continues.

I'm 7 stone actually, not that it makes any difference, because I could still strip a pair of cuffs off, plastic or not, and be all over them like a fucking seagull on a chip before they could say "plasti-cuffs" again, so I sit back in relative safety, retreating inwards, listening, assessing, gauging and settle in for the journey.

CHAPTER 4

We're here now, and I flinch in mock terror when the pillowcase is pulled off my head.

I don't know where 'here' is but I know it's west from where I was picked up, and after counting down the minutes and gauging the average speed I can tell we're about 11 miles away. I also know this place is like a fortress. Gate after gate after gate, and armed men patrolling, checking and watching. Ooh fucking scary: NOT! I subconsciously look for exits, hiding places, and a way out, but to say the odds are stacked against an escape is an understatement. They're cemented, reinforced and held in place with fuck off iron girders.

A shift in the atmosphere now. The two police officers are quiet, alert and have their 'game' faces on as we head into what looks like a sprawling Dockyard.

There are buildings everywhere. Small white sheds, single storey porta cabins, shipping containers, sky-high warehouses, and everything in between. We pass another gate with the ubiquitous gatehouse and a couple of surly looking guards onto a runway. Now my interest is piqued. A runway? In the middle of a dockyard? Alarm bells are ringing!

We approach another strange looking building and stop at a set of roller shutter doors, waiting for them to open as sleet starts to fall from the sky.

Once inside I subconsciously run through the exits, chokepoints, guards, weapons, size, and myriad other things, committing them to memory, until I see a man. A man I've seen before. A man who very few have seen and lived to tell the tale. An unremarkable man to say the least. Someone you'd probably forget just as easily. But I NEVER forget...

'The hidden vaults of the human brain contain vast, almost limitless information. Everything we have seen, heard, felt, experienced is within that vault. Every word spoken, by us or someone else, every place we've been, every face we've seen. Emotions, memories, tastes, smells, facts, knowledge. All of it, seemingly out of reach, save for a small percentage of it. Total recall would seem impossible, but impossible is actually I'm possible spelt differently and centuries of practice have shown me how, and to me it's as simple as pressing 'play' on the scene I want then sitting back to enjoy the show.

Mr Menji: An effeminate-looking Asian man. Owner of Mencorp - a massive tech ware company involved in everything from wind-up radios to Artificial intelligence. Unremarkable in many respects but his name is only spoken in hushed tones.

He is a man of many 'talents' if you can call drug-harvesting, drug-distribution, people trafficking, prostitution, kidnap, mass genocide, arms dealing, and organised crime talents.

I can still remember the first time I saw him, what he was wearing, exactly what he said and that he is pure evil. The policemen and guards alike cower subconsciously at the very presence of him and I follow suit hoping he hasn't mastered total recall and recognised me.

"What have we here then?" He demands, looking at the policemen who have now gripped my arms tighter.

"New stock Mr Menji"

"New stock indeed officer. Very pretty for a boy. Too valuable for the original purpose. Our 'friends' overseas would like him very much"

"Er? Too valuable? I'm sorry Mr Menji, we don't want any part of that. We... well, we all know what overseas means. And we... er, we only provide runners, not ch..."

And that's as far as he gets, as Menji bursts forward with lightning speed and buries a Tanto up to the hilt in his throat - fucking good shot cunto!

Nobody reacts. Nobody dares to react, as the policeman's legs seem to crumple like paper and he collapses on the spot and Mr Menji stares challengingly at those in the room.

"Now, as I was saying, he IS very pretty and he WILL be well received by our 'friends' overseas. Now, tête-à-tête over. Get him cleaned up please" He chirps in a sing-song voice, seemingly oblivious to the murder he's just committed.

The guy's a fucking psycho!

CHAPTER 5

The average human uses only 20-30 percent of their strength, and prime athletes maybe 40-50 percent. This is because our brain cannot receive all the messages sent by protein cells or muscle cells in general at once. We are theoretically 8 times stronger than chimpanzees, though chimps are stronger than us since they have access to most cells in their bodies and they can receive most neuron waves sent to the brain, whereas humans cannot.

But - and it's a big but - under acute stress, the body's sympathetic nervous system prepares the body for sustained, vigorous action. The adrenal glands dump cortisol and adrenaline into the blood stream. Blood pressure surges and the heart races, delivering oxygen and energy to the muscles. It's the biological equivalent of opening the throttle of an engine.

Under these conditions people are capable of incredible feats of strength. For example: the Mother who can lift a car clean off her child, or the father who can hold the entire weight of a crumbling two storey house while his family make their escape.

Sounds like an X-men film doesn't it? Sounds unreal doesn't it? Well it's true, I know this because I can tap into it at will, and when I open the floodgates my 7 stone frame could tear King-Kong limb from limb!

So here I am, in a shipping crate! I shit you not!

I'm in an actual shipping crate. Covered in itchy fucking sawdust from the 4 holes they drilled for me to breathe through after piping in what smelled and tasted like Sevoflurane. Oh, and this lovely little shipping crate is in a fucking gigantic steel shipping container with lots of other crates full of snivelling children. To say I'm not impressed is an understatement, so by channelling that Adrenalin/cortisol cocktail I turn into a smaller, angrier, pink version of The Incredible Hulk and I'm out of the crate in seconds and looking for somebody to slay... Except there's nobody here, well, nobody except the other children who have obviously heard the noise of splintering wood, but are probably unaware of me.

It would be so easy to open all the crates in here, force the door of the shipping container open and then kill every cunt on board before piloting this ship to somewhere safe and secure, but I don't make rash decisions. It's this methodical, analytic approach that has seen me safely through the centuries, so I do the exact opposite.

Tipping my crate over and stamping on it, I move it to the door end of the container, where I crawl back inside after cutting my forehead and smearing the blood over my face to make it look as though the rough seas have thrown the crate from its original location and deposited an unconscious me and a battered box into a heap on the floor. There I lie and wait, formulating a plan until my equilibrium is disturbed as the ship starts to slow and voices shout. I can feel the chill in the air now as we come to a standstill, then a crane starts up, chains are rattled and the shipping container is taken from the boat onto what I assume is dry land.

More shouts follow, accompanied by that hollow clanging sound associated with locks being slid back. Light floods in and a deep baritone voice asks "Qué es esto?" Spanish. "la caja esta abierta!" Followed by a thick Mancunian accent "yer, I can see that our kid. It's obviously fallen off ain't it? It 'as been at sea ain't it?"

"My boss no be happy with damaged goods"

"What damage? The friggin' box? Come on!"

"No, the boy. The boy cut. Maybe dead?"

"Fer fuck's sake mate! I'll check 'im over!"

And so I'm dragged from the box and 'checked' by having my head twisted about while 'Manc' looks at my eyes, the cut on my forehead, and in my ears. "Alright our kid?" He asks. "Hey! You ok mate?. You English? Oh! Mate!" I adjust my focus to take in the dockside we're on and mumble the answers to his questions. "See? Perfect. Now let's get these crates unloaded. This dickhead can ride in the cab seeing as his box is fucking broke!"

And that's it. Literally. I'm shoved in the cab with explicit warnings that if I try and escape or fuck about I'll be shot and chucked in the sea for the fish to eat, while they unload the other crates, and very soon we're motoring down the right hand side of a road passing Spanish road signs through hills to what looks like a huge onion-domed palace.

CHAPTER 6

He's not a bad sort! That's what they said,

In with the wrong crowd, just easily led,

Well that was then and this is now,

A knife in your pocket, a scowl on your brow,

Looking for targets, someone to beat,

Start with a fist, end with your feet,

Fuck the police! I ain't afraid of the law,

My Dad's a smack head, my Mum's a whore,

Outside the shops whatever the season,

I'll knock you out for no fucking reason,

My ego huge, my brain much smaller,

Hoodlum, gangster, bad-boy, brawler,

This is My England, and I'm so patriotic,

Dangerous, drugged-up, and fucking psychotic,

You got something nice -I want it - I'll take it,

Stick your nose in and I'll fucking break it!

Most men are cunts, all women are bitches,

If I fancy a laugh, you'll be leaving in stitches,

I'm the end result when shit breeds with shit,

On the streets of your country, get used to it!

Bobby digs was a lorry driver. Overweight, powerfully built, overworked, underpaid and dangerous! Reliable, ruthless, and on the take. Known to his friends as Digger; he liked a full English breakfast, a can of Stella or two, Burberry check, and a fucking good scrap! A gold-plated shithead, but he could keep a secret, especially when he was being paid to do so. So when he was approached by one of his fellow drivers and offered a 'shitload of cash' to do a bit of driving over on the continent he was happy to do so, in fact he was deliriously happy to do so.

Bobby had of late acquired a new pastime; snorting cocaine like it was going out of fashion.

CHAPTER 7

We arrive at the 'onion palace' to another gaggle of guards and 'Manc' has just enough time to snort a line of cocaine and brush his teeth with the remnants before the gates open to allow us entry into a well-lit court-yard full of luxury cars. There are Porsche's, Bentley's, Mercedes, Tesla's and the perfunctory Range Rovers parked up with drivers stationed in the climate controlled cabins awaiting someone or something. The crates and I are unloaded into a huge marquee, one lot by a forklift truck, and me by a wild-eyed Mancunian with a Burberry cap and a bad attitude. "Digger laaaad!!" Comes a voice out of the darkness as 'Manc' turns around with a full-face scowl. "Ok our Kid? What the fuck you doin' here like?" He demands. "Clean up Bobby. We gotta get these fucking kids clean and shit for the auction innit?"

"Here. Start with this little cunt" he orders before shoving me in the general direction of the new arrival. "See you at the Derby Sunday our kid?"

"Yeah, bring some tools. It's gonna be fuckin' epic!"

After being checked by a nervous-looking Doctor who keeps making subtle facial expressions at me (fuck. I know I'm good, but I haven't mastered mind reading yet!), I'm put with the rest of the children to be washed, scrubbed, have my make-up done (really) and then dressed in smart clean clothes ready for the 'auction' to start.

The auction consists of dozens of children locked in cages, whilst those interested peruse, ask questions and take note of our numbers. There are many buyers here. Many are childless and looking for someone to call their own. The children chosen by them may or may not be destined for a life of happiness, but many more buyers are sexual predators or murderers and I can see it in their eyes. The children chosen by them are not destined for a life of happiness. They are destined to suffer!

The caged children are now almost aware of their fate and are crying and pleading to be let go. Some of the more switched on are smashing their faces against the mesh cages, knowing the sexual predators won't want ugly, and scarred children, whilst some just sit there resigned to their fate. Me? I just stand there shaking in mock-fear, looking shocked and sad, waiting till the auction is over.

I don't have to wait too long as it winds down naturally. It appears that most of the kids are sold, some have bashed themselves unconscious and some have been sent elsewhere to be disposed of. To say I'm angry, pissed off, and sickened is an understatement, as I sit in my cage waiting for the right moment to strike!

CHAPTER 8

J ack Daniel (Whiskey to his mates) was 33 years old. An ex-squaddie who'd joined the British Army as a boy soldier 17 years earlier in the Parachute Regiment. He'd worked alongside many elite regiments like The SBS, The SAS, Russia's Spetsnaz, and even America's Delta Force, yet here he was 5 years into 'Civvy Street' working a shit job, packing stuff into boxes and hating every second of it. His mates still serving kept asking him "what's it like? I bet you're raking it in aren't you?" keen to know what to expect, but Jack had been an excellent soldier, straight as a die, and an honourable man. In short, he couldn't lie to his mates.

"No, it's shit" he would say. "Killing people, gathering intelligence, training soldiers, toppling regimes, and being part of a huge tight-knit family doesn't transfer to civvy life!"

He didn't particularly miss the bureaucracy and all the mither of the army, but he did miss the camaraderie and the sense of belonging. The sense that he was making a difference, and a sense that the millions of pounds spent training him was being put to good use.

He'd tried to scratch that itch by becoming a bouncer, then a debt-collector, then a bodyguard, but it was no use. No use until he volunteered to become a Police Community Support Officer. Being a PCSO was a thankless task. All the grief from Joe Public, without the benefits of being an actual Police officer, all the shit, all the unsociable hours, the basic shit kit you were supposed to use - not a great job at all, but what it did give him was 'victims' - victims of crime to be more precise. Normal, everyday people who had been let down by the system. A system that offered help, understanding, and often compensation to those committing crimes, while largely ignoring the 'victims', which is where Jack came in; he avenged those wrongs, he stood up for those without a voice, he collated information about criminals and their heinous crimes, he logged details in his head (never on paper or digital media) of the scum which was turning the country, his country, into a cesspool of drug dealers, gangsters, thieves, rapists, and things too sick even to name. He logged those details, logged, planned, and executed: literally!

He'd kept a mental tally of those he'd killed, maimed, and scared the shit out of and he was currently at 87. He always remembered number one especially: a wealthy barrister who'd successfully prosecuted many of the country's ne'er-do-well's only to be failed by the very law she herself fought to uphold. Her name was Ellen and she'd been stalked, kidnapped, and raped by the pond-life she'd successfully thrown the book at a decade earlier. When Jack met her she had barely been functioning. Bitter, twisted and as it happened a widow of one of the lads he'd served with on several tours. Right there and then they'd formed an alliance, an understanding, and a pact to do their bit to rid the world of the 'undesirables' commonly found in today's society; 48 hours later the pond-life was dead - Jack's first kill as a civilian.

CHAPTER 9

"Tired! So tired I could shit and fall over in it" Digger moaned out loud. "Time for some fucking Charlie I reckon Mr Digs." Baggie, blade, rolled up note and a snort or three later and he wasn't so tired anymore, but ready for some fun. The sort of 'fun' he'd had with that slag a couple of weeks ago. Stuck up bitch. "I'm actually doing law. Following in my Aunt's footsteps" she'd boasted to some lads. Yeah! Well I'll be doing you later, he thought. And he was. Bobby Digs, infamous bad boy, jack of all trades, balls-deep in some toffee-nosed slag who'd be waking up with sore holes and the after effects of a Gin and Rohypnol cocktail. Trouble was, he didn't know where to start looking. He was in some fucking poncy stately home thing with no women except the hired help, and he wasn't stupid enough to shit on his own doorstep. No, he thought. I'll get pissed and wait till I'm back home with a pocket full of Rohypnol before I fuck another bit of posh totty. And that's what he thought. He knew he could get away with it again. He knew he could just take whoever he wanted. Knew the silly bitches would remember it. Knew they'd believe they had consented. He knew exactly what he was doing. But what he didn't know was he was a marked man. Bobby Digs was on Whiskey's list. He wouldn't know what hit him.

CHAPTER 10

U s kids are sent to the 'infirmary' to be checked over by the medical team to ensure the bidder's latest purchases are fit, healthy and disease-free. We are still in cages with invoices stuck to them and I grimace at my 'worth' which is a measly $65,000 and wonder why the fuck everything in this world has to be americanised!? It's cold, sterile and clinical in the infirmary as we all sit and wait for the staff to work their way down the rows of cages. I notice that we're all being given the good news by some fucking meat-head with a tranquilliser gun before our check-ups to keep us compliant and incapable of putting up a fight, so I flood my system with adrenalin and endorphins to counter the drugs about to be pumped into me and pretend to be unconscious whilst I'm jabbed, poked and robbed of 5ml of my precious blood. At close range I notice the Dr following in the meat-head's wake is the same one making subtle eye movements to me earlier that day and wonder what the fuck he was trying to convey and realise he's left the lock off my cage.

Once Dr Kildare and the meat-head fuck off I can maybe have a snoop around and put my plan into action, the plan I haven't actually fucking made up yet. 12: you're a bell end sometimes!

Once I'm sure it's clear I open my typically fucking bastard cunting creaking door!! And QUIETLY make my way around the infirmary checking on all the other kids who are still drugged but thankfully breathing. I find the exit, check my surroundings, stick my ear to the door and listen carefully with my mouth open to drown out my own internal noise. All seems clear so I make my way into the adjoining corridor.

The corridor is long, dimly lit and surprisingly Spartan, on my left side are rows of doors with numbers on them. On my right is a huge garage containing cars, motorbikes and what looks like a cash in transit van. Maybe I can find a big fuck off spanner in there? Well, I could have if there wasn't CCTV everywhere! Ah well, hand to hand it is then.

I silently head down the corridor listening and watching as I arrive at the first door marked as Cantina. I stop and listen to the voice coming from inside "No te preocupes. estaré allí" no other voices, I'll make an educated guess he's on the phone. Slowly I open the door waiting for a reaction, but unfortunately there's no other way to do this and I smile as I'm met with the view of a guard with his back to me pouring hot water into a bowl of noodles. I check our immediate surroundings, then happy it's safe to do so I rise, approach and smash a fuck- off ridged hand into his Brachial nerve before dragging his prone body out of sight and cable tying him tightly to a chair hoping the cable ties are so tight his fucking fingers will drop off!

I make sure the door is locked after sticking the cleaning in progress sign just outside it and wake up my new mate with his own bowl of hot noodles.

His first expression is one of pain as he realises he's covered in hot noodles, closely followed by fear, closely followed by a slightly bemused look that it's only a kid stood in front of him that looks like Justin fucking Bieber!

He immediately starts gobbing off in Spanish thinking: I'm an adult, he's a kid, I'll bollock him and he'll do as he's told, etc. etc. Same old same old to me, but he needs to know I'm fucking dangerous and we need to set the tempo here so his newest expression is one of terror and searing pain as I detach his calf with the fork from his ruined bowl of noodles and start asking him questions about layout, security, staff and anything else that'll help me navigate my way through this godforsaken place, which he's more than happy to answer once I motion to his other calf with my 'surgical' fork.

So with my newly acquired weapon, information and a mental image of the layout I leave him with the helpful advice of PRICE: Protection, Rest, Ice, Compression, and Elevation, oh and another smack on the chin!

CHAPTER 11

Whiskey was rubbing his hands together for two reasons: one, because it was a bit chilly in the mountains of the Sierra Nevada, Two, because he had the good fortune to be in this beautiful part of the world, with next to no CCTV and a police force that wouldn't even bat an eyelid when some piece of shit English lorry driver went missing.

He was well-equipped, well-versed in the environment, and as the 'kids' would say – well-excited about number 88 (Robert Anthony digs) who had well-overstayed his welcome on planet earth by raping Ellen's niece.

He'd tailed his latest target for days, and couldn't quite believe his luck when he heard he was off abroad for 'a bit of work for some dodgy fuckers'. So with a days' grace Whiskey had called in a few favours and managed to get a seat on an old mucker's Cessna which he'd jumped out of weighed down with kit, 10 clicks from the flashing tracker he'd installed on number 88's phone.

He could have shot the aforementioned piece of shit from a kilometre away, maybe even rigged his lorry up with explosives, or gone all James Bond and cut his brake lines, but this was personal and he wanted Robert Anthony Digs to know why he was being disembowelled and strangled with his own intestines. He wanted him to know he was going to die. He wanted him to suffer. He wanted him to know there was no place on this earth for those who take pleasure in defiling women for no other reason than their own sick pleasure. And he'd also spotted a kid that looked like Justin Bieber being prodded and shoved by the soon- to-be dead Mancunian shitbag and it made him shiver with disgust!

CHAPTER 12

Bobby was lying on the bed in his room with a towel around his waist having pulled one off to the porn his mate Herbie had sent him. Herbie always sent him some random shit; porn, horrific accidents, funny stuff, and executions. He was laughing at some poor fucker who'd just been flayed with a cane when there was a tap on his door.

"Coming" he shouted, with a little grin at his choice of words. "Giz a sec, I'm just puttin' some duds on!" He opened the door, rubbing his nostrils to clear any Charlie away, and the last thing he saw was a blue spark before everything went black.

The coldness of the water took Bobby's breath away as he woke up bollock-naked with his own pants in his mouth and cable ties around his neck, wrists and ankles.

"wha, wha, wha, what the fuck!" he screamed through his impromptu gag, before noticing the biggest man he'd ever seen standing in front of him. This fucker was about 7ft judging by how close his head was to the ceiling, muscly as fuck too, with pale blue eyes that stared through him into his soul and a wicked-looking knife in his hand.

Bobby gulped, gagged on his pants and pissed himself, in that order.

"Dirty Bastard!" came the response from the behemoth in front of him. "Know who I am?" Bobby shook his head. "I've come all the way from England to see you. Thought we'd have a chat before we start the Blood Eagle. You know what the Blood Eagle is Bobby?" Bobby shook his head again. "It's a ritualised method of execution made infamous by the Vikings of all people. They used to sever the ribs from the spine with a sharp tool and pull the lungs through the opening to create a pair of 'wings'. Bloody painful old lad. Takes a while to kill you too. Quite a bit of work involved as well, but I don't mind, because as the beautiful girls on the L'oreal adverts would say: 'Because you're worth it'. And you know all about beautiful girls don't you Bobby? Beautiful girls who can't say no to your charm and the fucking Rohypnol you put in their drinks eh Bobby? Girls who are bright, intelligent, and have a great future ahead of them in law. Girls whose lives are now ruined because of wankers like you Bobby!"

Bobby was shaking uncontrollably now "mmf! Mmmfmff! Mmmummm!"

"Pardon Bobby? Just about to tell me I've got it wrong? It wasn't you? You don't know what I'm talking about? Well, Mr Robert Anthony Digs, I'm not the type of man who makes mistakes with stuff like this. I wouldn't have jumped out of a perfectly good plane weighed down with guns, ammunition and this lovely, shiny FUCKING sharp knife if I wasn't absolutely sure you're the piece of shit I'm looking for. However, what I'm not entirely sure about is what's going on here? Lots of nice cars, lots of crates, lots of money, lots of armed guards. So.... I AM going to kill you. I AM going to use this lovely, shiny FUCKING sharp knife to Blood Eagle you, and I AM going to enjoy it. BUT... if you tell me what's going on here I WILL kill you quickly. So? Ready to answer?"

Bobby was nodding his head like a thing possessed. Crying and nodding. Emptying his bladder and nodding. Voiding his bowels and nodding. Vomiting and nodding.

"They're sick mate! Fucking sick! I didn't know it was kids. Honestly. It's for drugs or something. Fucking sick bastards! I can help you. I can show you. They know me! They know me! I can get you past the security! I can Mmmff" He pleaded as his pants were stuffed back in his mouth.

"Enough chat for now" Whiskey whispered. "Do I look like I need your help to get past these rent-a-guards? I've killed three of them already so we could have this chat. So now I'm going to ask a few questions. I want answers. Just answers. No bargaining. No pleading. Just answers. Got it?"

Bobby started the whole crying, shitting, pissing, nodding routine again.

Whiskey pulled the gag out again and continued "how many kids are here?"

"I can show y....."

Crack!! A sharp pain followed as Bobby's head split open from the strike with the knife's pommel and the pants were shoved back in his mouth.

"Not too good at this are you Bobby? Just answers I said. Just answers."

15 minutes later Whiskey had the answers he needed and Robert Anthony Digs had sprouted a pair of wings. Oh, and Whiskey had lied about killing him quickly!

CHAPTER 13

S it rep: 3 guards neutralised. Fork in waistband. Glock 17 acquired, and a tearful Dr Kildare looking down the business end of that marvel of Austrian engineering whilst jabbering away.

"Please, you have to help me, you can get out, raise the alarm. Please. They have my family. I saw you weren't in a box like the others. You've seen it all. Please. Go. Tell someone. I can help you."

"I don't need help" I reply. "How do I know you're not talking shit? How do I know you're not one of them? I don't know fuck all about you! You could be setting me up. You fucking jabbed me with a needle you twat!"

"I, I, I, erm... It was saline solution! I knew your cage Number and put saline in your shot. Please, help me! I'll give you anything. Anything you want. You want money? Drugs? Treatment? Are you hurt? Please!"

You can tell a lot about a person by their eyes, and I knew Dr Kildare was telling the truth. "What's your name?"

"Dr Green" he replied. Fuck it, I still prefer Kildare.

"Ok, I'll help you then. But if you cross me I'll plunge one of those fucking syringes in your eye, ok? Now, tell me everything I need to know."

"They're selling kids" he started, "to rich people, people who want them for everything from raising them as their own, to sick individuals with snuff films and stuff in mind. They're operating above the law in the UK. They've got judges, MP's, famous people, rich people, loads of people, just people everywhere" he continued, with tears rolling down his cheeks. "They prey on homeless or poor kids. Offer them money to shift drugs at first, then if they're gullible or fit a certain profile they're shipped over to Europe where people trafficking is rife and the authorities are either threatened or paid to turn the other cheek! I, I heard about it through a fellow paediatrician and thought I could help. I thought I could go to my boss. Thought he'd listen. He bloody listened alright. Listened and told the Chinese psychopath whose whole bloody idea this is. Kidnapped my bloody family, brought them here as a reminder that I have an important job to do for this... this bloody, bloody sick regime!"

I had to smile to myself, his Wife and kids were being held hostage, he was being forced to work against his will, and the strongest language he could conjure up was 'bloody'. Fuck that! These people were gold-plated cuntfucks of the highest spunking, shitting order, and that was putting it mildly. "So? I get all that, but where do I start? Where are the ringleaders of this shit-show? I've seen plenty of the fuckers, I just need to know where they will be now. Them and the hired-help."

"The village, they call it the village. Loads of lodges and hot tubs and, and, and the guards too. They've got quarters for the guards too" he blurted, before giving me all the information I hoped I'd need. So after giving him a final warning not to fuck me over I can get on with my favourite bit: giving folks the good news, and doing it quietly. I fucking love my job and I've already decided lethal force is the way forward for any of the fuckers involved in this sick shit. Children are the future of this world; weirdo's, paedo's and psychos are NOT so fucking look out!

I make my way into the populated area where the sick fuckers with the money are staying in sheer opulence and luxury, surrounded by armed guards, whilst most of the kids are still out of it or even worse, aware of their fate.

I'm angry, buzzing with Adrenalin and ready to go.

Victim one is a big fucker. All tattoos and attitude with a suppressed MP5, a Fairbarn Sykes fighting knife, and anger radiating from every pore. I approach silently from behind and leap onto his back whilst simultaneously sticking the scalpel Dr Kildare had given me into his carotid artery, sawing and pushing forward through his Adam's apple, not that slice across the throat shit you see in the films! He was fucking brown bread before he hit the deck and kindly left the knife and the MP5 to me in his will. So now I have everything I need to wage a war on any fucker that stands in my way!

CHAPTER 14

M r Menji was in his apartment, above the peasants who'd flocked to his auction being fed grapes by the busty blonde he'd recently added to his harem.
She was beautiful, fit and alluring. 'Could maybe use a bit of silicone in her breasts' he thought, as she fed herself one of the grapes before asking "ready to go again my master?"

He loved being in control. He loved being feared. He loved being obeyed. He loved money, power, and all the trappings that came with it. He thought back to his humble beginnings as a fisherman's son in the tiny little village where everybody either lived on their junks or in mud and bamboo huts. He remembered the very moment his life had changed forever.

He was just 12 years old when they came. Men. Hard-faced men. Guns and gold. They came looking for children for the black market. Children taken from their families, sometimes for money, sometimes in payment for 'protection' from the gangs. Sometimes just abducted without their parents knowledge. Menji was one of the fortunate ones, his family had received a payment for him. He was already an excellent fisherman at 12 years old and was deemed fearless, often going out into the turbulent waters where no one else would dare to venture. He was strong and well-built too, with a reputation as a bit of a scrapper, so he'd quickly caught the eye of the 'Boss' who'd requisitioned him personally. Menji, in turn, had slit the Boss's throat that night, stolen his gold, killed the other 11 men in the gang, and made his way to Hong Kong with a bag full of gold and a dream.

He'd risen quickly through the ranks of the organised crime syndicates by being both ruthless and fearless, killing any and all who got in his way.

He'd invested heavily in business and property and was worth billions of dollars with his fingers in many a pie. He owned companies, islands, aircraft, yachts, politicians and police forces. He was rich, untouchable, and about to make use of the Viagra again with his beautiful blonde 'assistant'.

CHAPTER 15

Whiskey was confused. He was sure he was seeing things.

He was sure he'd just seen Justin Bieber almost cut some fucker's head off!

He shook his head, had a gulp of water and shoved a Mars bar in his gob. Nah! Couldn't be! Come on old lad!

He was making his way around the accommodation area - silent, watchful, poised and deadly. He'd got the mental image of the lay-out in his head and was heading to where the recently deceased Mr Digs had told him the kids were being held, when he spotted movement ahead. He stayed hidden in the shadows and took in the scene through the Leupold scope attached to his rifle.

There were guards stationed around what looked like log cabins. Some of them bored and disinterested, some of them switched on and focussed, and one in particular with a kid on his back and a knife in his neck.

He stayed silent and continued to watch as the kid dispatched the guard with ruthless efficiency and dragged the twitching corpse into the undergrowth. Not possible he thought, 7 stone kids don't drag 20 stone men backwards through undergrowth one handed! He needed to get down there and see what the fuck was going on, so off he set, keeping to the shadows with his rifle on a tactical chest harness and his suppressed Glock in his hand, moving with an equal measure of speed and stealth. He reached the first of the guards which turned out to be two. Thinking quickly he threw a pebble in the opposite direction to gauge the guards' responses and was rewarded with a short nod from one to the other to check it out: fucking amateurs!

Guard two was trying to do an impression of a soldier by tip-toeing round the corner to where the pebble had landed, whilst guard one was lighting up his cigarette and ruining any night vision he may have had. Whiskey stepped in front of him and broke his neck. He was dead before he'd taken a drag on his cigarette. Guard two was back within 15 seconds and stage-whispering to his mate "where are ya? I can smell the cigarette smoke. Crash me a ciggy will ya?" he made his way to a cigarette-butt littered wooden gazebo still moaning about guarding 'these rich cunts' when he felt Whiskey's forearm around his throat and heard a whispered "how many guards?". "14 including me and me mate" came the reply "with more inside. You're fucked mate". "Make that 12 now" Whiskey grunted as he snapped the guards' neck.

12 guards, more inside but just one of me he thought – piece of piss! And on he went, ready to kill each and every one of them. Less backup for those inside he reasoned as he opened the flood-gates of his fury.

CHAPTER 16

I'd just dragged the big cunt with no Adam's apple into the undergrowth when I went all 'Peter fucking Parker' and my spider senses started tingling: I could sense there was somebody watching me and so I melted into the night to lie still and watch. Turns out I was right as an even bigger fucker appears after a while with the look of murder on his face. Friend or foe? Dunno, but he's just snapped two guards' necks like fucking cocktail sticks, which reminds me – I'm fucking Hank Marvin. Not actually fucking the lead guitarist of The Shadows as in having you know...? but, er... Fuck off! I'm 12 and straight and even if I was going to be shagging somebody (which I'm not) it'd be somebody like, er... well it wouldn't be a lead guitarist.

Or a bloke.

Or anybody famous (probably) unless they were tidy and not too old.

But older than me.

Well, older than I look if you know what I men? No, not men. Mean, I mean mean.

Fuck me! Not literally (obviously).

I'm starving basically.

Well not actually starving, but hungry, very hungry and... Anyway, shut the fuck up now brain, that bigger fucker I was on about has just come into view and he looks professional and switched on so I guess I should follow suit.

I stay silent and watch as the man mountain moves like someone half his weight and size and makes his way down to where I was just stood, reading the landscape: the clever fucker is tracking me. Doing a good job too as he looks right over to where I am and pulls out a pair of fucking night vision goggles before snatching his head to the right and hitting the deck as someone else tries very un-fucking-successfully to move through the undergrowth without making a sound.

I wait patiently for Mr professional to make his move so I can Foxtrot Oscar out of here and continue on my merry way, but then I spot another fucking guard approaching from the other direction in what a professional would call a pincer movement, but these thick twats aren't professional, just lucky. I also notice he (guard number two, not Mr Professional) is wearing flip flops, and there's nothing I FUCKING hate more than men wearing flip flops. He's got to go. He absolutely, indubitably has to fucking go, so I tense, relax, flood my system with the magic formula and spring like a fucking gazelle at Mr Fucking flip fucking flop ready to fucking fuck him up. I hit him so hard and fast he leaves terra firma and his flip flops fly off as he lands with an unnaturally angled neck, dead as a Dodo (which I believe I've actually seen) as Mr Pro (I'm bored of saying professional now) stands and throws his knife with an unerring efficiency into guard one's windpipe. We lock gazes, mine feral and aggressive, his almost kindly as he asks softly "are you ok mate? It's alright; I'm on your side. Come with me and I'll keep you safe"

I open my mouth to reply as I see a flash of light and my world goes black.

CHAPTER 17

A Taser is a battery-powered, handheld device which de-livers a short, low-energy electrical pulse. Two electrode wires are attached to the gun's electrical circuit. When one pulls the trigger it breaks open a compressed gas cartridge inside the gun and flings the electrodes into contact with a body and a charge flows into the muscles, and according to my memory banks, it delivers 19 short pulses per second over 5 seconds, with an average current of 2 milliamps. It creates an electric field, which stimulates nerve cells called alpha motor neurons to send an electrical impulse. The im-pulse travels to muscles and causes short, sustained muscle contractions.

It has two modes: the first, pulse mode, causes neurom-uscular incapacitation as the neural signals that control muscles become uncoordinated, and muscles contract at random. The second mode, drive-stun, uses pain to get com-pliance.

The most common side effects are pain, bruising and two little fucking marks like Dracula has been feasting on you. So basically when I woke up I was fucking sore. Sore and angry until my training kicked in and I became the foppish, small child with tear-stained cheeks they expected to see. A child that had been Tasered AND drugged. Poor little me!

I took in my surroundings and allowed myself a wry little smile. I was in a cage again, suspended from the ceiling of the garage I'd spotted earlier. Mr Pro was in a similar predicament opposite me but appeared to be unconscious still and the buyers I'd seen at the auction were all in attendance too.

"Awake at last 'Boy'?" Came a voice from above me.

"Caused me some upset haven't you Boy" he whispered matter of factly, placing great emphasis on the 'Boy' part.

"Who'd have thought a 'Boy' could upset this equilibrium so easily hey? A mere 'Boy' escaping his cage, attacking one of my men and then terrorising my good Dr Green into letting him go again. But you're not a 'Boy' are you 12? Not an ordinary 'Boy' anyway. You're my greatest success so far 12" he continued.

"Do you know why you're 12? You probably think it's because you're 12 years old don't you? Ha ha. No! You're 12 because you're my twelfth 'experiment'. The twelfth child taken from the streets. The twelfth child with the correct genetics. The perfect genetics for my team to work with. 12 has always been my lucky number. Very poignant to me. 12 was my age when I killed 12 men. 12 was the number of years it took me to reach the pinnacle of success within the dark underbelly of organised crime. 12 is how many billions of dollars I'm worth. Yes! 12 is indeed my lucky number!" He roared, veins bulging in his neck.

"You don't know though do you? You just think 12 is your name because....? Because it was programmed into your brain along with all the other nonsense floating around there. Faux-memories of Egyptians you've lived alongside. Programmed snippets of lost eons spent honing your skills and trying to live a 'normal' life. Whilst thinking that you don't belong. And the icing on the cake is this: it's been 12 weeks since you were 'programmed'! How coincidental is that?" He added with a flourish and a fake bow.

"Oh.. And.." he laughed "you actually think it's real! How fucking ridiculous is that? You think you're immortal, or a comic book character, or one of the heroes in those 'games' you play. Those online games on the very consoles my company mass produces and fills with subliminal messages and mind-altering technology, and then you proudly tell people you're a 'gamer. How completely ridiculous! Not just that you believe this parallel universe I have created in your head, but the whole idea that you're a 'gamer' because you play games.

I actually have people put 'gamer' on their CV's when they look to be employed by me. What do you say to that 'Boy'?"

I return his fake smile.

"I concur. Completely ridiculous. I mean, if you watched a lot of TV in your leisure time then you wouldn't call yourself a 'TV'er' would you? Or if you masturbated a lot you wouldn't add 'Wanker' to your list of interests would you?"

"Incidentally, does it say 'fucking sociopather' on your CV? Because it's a dead giveaway. I mean; you've only got to be near you for 10 minutes to see you're completely fucking mad" I continue, trying to force some confidence into my voice, though he has got me wondering. And panicking. And I never fucking panic!

"You'll be wandering around with tin foil on your head soon shouting "gibbery gibbery, I'm a china teapot", so don't talk shit to me about silly notions you can create memories in people's heads you utter fucking bell end!"

"Oh, how absolutely refreshing!" he replies gleefully. "Somebody who doesn't kiss my arse. Someone who actually has some balls to argue with me. This 'Boy' has more backbone than most of you cunts here" he continues with a wave of his arm in the direction of his guards. "My protégé.

The first of his kind.

My greatest success.

Virtual reality on steroids.

But don't worry all, he won't be breaking out of this cage. He's had a dose of Metoprolol to go with his Propofol".

"So? Who would like an upgrade for their latest purchase?" he asked the room full of buyers. "Bring your cheque books and we'll retire to the banqueting suite"

CHAPTER 18

"**S**o, is it true?" whispered Mr Pro. We are still in our respective cages in a now empty room. Me shaking with a tear in my eye. Him with a determined glint in his as he works at the lock on his cage.

"Which bit?" I reply. "The bit about me being superhuman, or the bit about me being an experiment? An electronically fucking brainwashed experiment at that!"

"Yeah, my name is 12. At least that's what I call myself. And I have been around for a while. More than the 12 weeks that twat said I have anyway. I know stuff. I know how to do things. Well, I think I do, or are they memories too?"

"Must have short-circuited me too then mate because I saw you in action. I saw you nearly cut some fucker's head off with a scalpel. I saw you drag that same fucker into the bushes one handed and I've been around for a long time. Never seen anything like that before though. Yeah, I've seen shitloads of people killed but not as efficiently as that. And as for a 12 year old 'kid' dragging a 20 stone bloke one handed like he's a fucking hotel pillow... well, if that's what a short-circuit can do then fucking sign me up".

"Maybe you've been zapped too?" I asked. "He knew loads of shit about me. I have got memories, if that's what they are, of some weird eons-ago shit that happened, but maybe that's all part of this virtual reality bollocks he was talking about. But, I know one thing; once we're out of here I'm going to kill that twat!"

"Anyway" he countered, "if you've been gone for the 12 weeks he mentioned why haven't I seen your face on the news or on posters? It's bollocks mate. He's pushing the right buttons that's all. Want me to pick your lock? Mine's done" he asked as he opened his door and swung his legs down.

"May as well. He's fucked me up with drugs apparently"

3 minutes later and we're both stood on the floor of the garage. "I'm Whiskey" he offers. "I'm 12" I reply.

"Ready to fuck some people up then 12?"

"Reckon I could be persuaded Whiskey"

So we set off, back into the centre of this den of iniquity, stopping to check out the exhibition in the room next door which consists of armour, battle axes, spears, flintlock pistols and a big fuck off longbow!

I smile as I lift it off the display stand and grab the quiver of arrows. "I'm having the longbow Mr Pro!"

"Who?"

"Mr Pro. That's you" I reply. "Well you're Whiskey now, but it's what I do. I assign names to people. You're Mr Pro because you look like a professional."

"Thanks for the compliment."

"You're welcome! The Doc is Dr Kildare, even though he's Dr Green. The lorry driver is Manc, because he's from Manchester."

"Was"

"Pardon?"

"Was. I said he was. From Manchester that is. He's fucking dead now though. Some 'Pro' has Blood eagled him."

"I'm impressed Mr Pr... Whiskey. Not many people know what the blood eagle is, let alone be mad enough to actually do it. Hah!

Wicked! Anyway. Everyone gets a nickname. Makes them easier to remember and quicker than describing them. Incidentally, do you know Tattoo?"

"Who?"

"Obviously not then. Can we get on with killing people now? I haven't fired a longbow for decades. Wonder if I've still got it?"

Whiskey allowed himself a smile. "Tell you what 12, you're fucking golden. Sure you can muster the strength to pull it back?"

"Fuck off. And anyway, it's draw, not pull. Plus my puny rhomboids, levator scapulae, and trapezius are more than capable of 'drawing' a bow this size thank you Mr Pro. So what you having then?"

Whiskey had to suppress a giggle. "Got to be that axe and the dagger I reckon."

"Let's Foxtrot Oscar then Mr Pro."

We head into the warren of corridors together this time and set to work making our way to the other kids, hoping I'll meet Menji and co along the way.

CHAPTER 19

The longbow is an extremely powerful, large bow and this one was taller than me, but any questions I may have had about carrying such a cumbersome weapon diminished once I'd nocked, drawn back, and put an arrow through the head of a guard from 100 metres away, taking him off his feet like he'd been hit by a Lion.

We make our way down to his twitching corpse and without even thinking about, I drag him one-handed out of sight and return to a smiling Whiskey. "What?"

"You've just done it again" he chuckles.

"Done what?"

"Dragged a bloke twice your weight one-handed like he was a fucking pillow."

I shrug "Oh yeah. Guess the drugs have worn off then." Before we move into a massive fuck off room full of caged kids and all hell breaks loose!

"No fucking guns!" Yells a voice. "You might hit the merchandise!"

Now that pisses me off. They're human beings, not fucking merchandise, and so we enter the fray, back to back, me already nocking and releasing and Whiskey weighing the axe in his massive meaty mitts.

"I want them alive but beaten!" Shouts the same voice from before, as dozens of armed men swarm the floor where we are about to unleash hell with Whiskey taking the first one to come into range's head clean off whilst I flood my system with the magic formula praying it still works before dropping the bow and pulling out two knives.

Everything seems to slow down for Whiskey. He swings the axe, cleaving skills and severing limbs whilst watching with awe as 12 goes to work, slicing and stabbing like a demented figure skater. Fingers are lopped off, stomachs are left gaping open, Achilles' tendons are sliced, causing bodies to fall everywhere only to be stomped upon and ruined. That kid is something else, he thinks, as the bodies pile up and are no longer replaced. But now Menji's personal security are closing in; 2 of them. Both steroid users-judging by their sheer size and demeanour- making even Whiskey look small and 12 tiny and insignificant.

They stop on the periphery and wait. No words are spoken, no words are needed. They're here to maim and capture Whiskey and 12 by any means necessary. "You take 'pretty boy' and I'll take 'Arnie'" mutters 12 as the two meat-heads beckon to draw them out, attacking ferociously as Whiskey and 12 clear the piles of bodies.

Whiskey parries 'pretty boys' punches and moves closer, stomping on his foot whilst delivering a palm-heel to his nose. His eyes water in response as he steps back and pulls a knife, knowing already that he's no match for Whiskey unarmed and slashes wildly. Whiskey lives for this shit: it's like being back in. The Adrenalin, the chance to pit your skills against another man. All the blood, sweat and tears. All the drills, all the sparring. Everything comes down to this. Nothing else exists. Just you and the obstacle before you, and so he grins as he waits for the blade to pass the point of no return before hammering his fist into 'pretty boys' olecranon breaking it and rendering his arm useless. Now he's shitting it. He's got one functional arm against a man of Whiskey's size and skill. Whiskey remembers an old mantra- 'it's not all physical: use your head'. So he does, he moves in and head-butts into 'pretty boys' face, making him 'ugly boy' as his nose collapses and he struggles to breathe, but to his credit he does manage to take a backswing which Whiskey ducks under before rising again with a brutal uppercut to 'ugly boys' chin, sending him crashing to the ground, and because this isn't some film where the audience are screaming at the good guy telling him the bad guy is still alive and about to rise once his back is turned, he wanders over to the recumbent form and breaks 'ugly boys' neck before turning to watch 12 and 'Arnie' go at it.

My system floods again with Adrenalin and Cortisol as the chemicals cause another chemical reaction and whether I'm an experiment or not is now irrelevant as I feel the change in me and charge at 'Arnie' putting every ounce of strength I have into a flying kick which sends every ounce of his synthetically-enhanced body flying backwards through the air 30 feet. Then I jump again and land on his chest and vent my anger on his face, landing a few good punches before a shot rings out and I roll to the side. Seconds later an arrow flies over my head and takes another of Menji's meat-heads off his feet. I look back and nod as Whiskey nocks another arrow whilst Menji and his men flee, then to prove a point, I pick 'Arnie' up and break his back over my knee.

CHAPTER 20

We clear the surrounding areas quickly and methodically before letting the kids out of their cages telling them to stay together and hide until Whiskey or I come for them. Now armed to the teeth we make our way through the rest of this god forsaken place finding small pockets of resistance which we deal with brutally and efficiently and I'm impressed with how silent and deadly Whiskey is for a big fucker, but there's still that question resonating through my mind: who am I!?

My train of thought is shattered by a familiar voice coming through the various intercom speakers positioned everywhere. "Thinking are you 'Boy'? Wondering? Yes, a neat trick with the Adrenalin and unlimited strength thing. I actually programmed that bit in myself. I mean, what's the use of being electronically enhanced if you have no 'super hero powers' ha ha ha ha!"

"So why don't you come and meet me face to face then? You can even bring a few of your meat-heads too if you want. Of course there's two fucking less now isn't there cunto!"

"Oh 12. You have a way with words. You always have I suppose. You were very vulgar when I found you, I did try to program it out but it's obviously deep-rooted. Maybe it's a by-product of being dumped by your parents, cast aside like an old keepsake which has lost its appeal. Those years on the street have been so unkind. Unlike me. Putting you up in one of my apartments. Oh, that view. Beautiful."

Now I'm fucking annoyed. "You're so full of shit you should be a fucking politician! You know nothing about me. NOTHING! Come on out and I'll show you all about being unkind you fucking freak!!"

"Ha ha ha. Touched a nerve have I 'Boy'? Well, I'll keep in touch. Just got to get the cargo loaded and I'll be back for another chat 'Boy'!"

I turn and vent my fury on a beefed up security door, kicking the living fuck out of it before Whiskey taps my shoulder. "Just check the combination lock. 1 and 7 show more signs of wear so we'll try them. It's normally four digits so that gives us 16 permutations. Watch yourself and I'll give it a try."

I respond through gritted teeth as he enters the correct combination and opens the door with a flourish. "I know that! I wasn't trying to fucking open it! I was venting! That utter cunt has wound me fucking up!"

Whiskey responds with an "ooh, somebody's tired!" As we enter the new room and subconsciously clear it.

"Security room" I whisper. "All the camera feeds and intercom are in here. One seat is still warm and the air has been disturbed. That fucker must have just been in here. Come on, we can catch him piece of piss" and then I notice the camera feed showing the room where all the kids are hiding as armed guards storm it and frog-march the kids out.

"Fucking stroll on!" I shout, as the fire alarm sounds and I see shutter after shutter falling on the screens in front of me.

54

CHAPTER 21

The kids are compliant enough after witnessing the armed men assail the room and then being prodded, threatened and cajoled with rifles, so the guards lead them out into the garage where any successful bidders who haven't fled in fear are waiting to receive them - which in all reality amounts to two. Two people who have paid money for a child to take and do whatever with. The rest are herded toward a lorry for resale at the next auction.

Gone are the reams of high-end cars, save for the German up-armoured SUV waiting for the new 'family' and Menji oversees the transaction smiling graciously as the couple stand there with huge grins on their faces. But Menji doesn't really actually care. He has the money in his accounts. Whether the child lives or dies is of no concern to him. Maybe they'll 'make it' like he did. Good luck to them if they do. It'd be even easier in today's society too. Much easier. Technology bridges the gap so easily. Video calls, social media, the dark web. All of it useful for nefariousness.

The kids are dumped unceremoniously in the waiting lorry, followed by a liberal dousing of Nitrous Oxide to keep them quiet and compliant, then they're off to the UK again to one of Menji's 'facilities' where their fate will be decided.

"All secure and ready to go when you are sir" nods one of his guards, surprised that Menji is actually travelling in the convoy with them.

"Very good. Are the explosives primed and timed?" He asks.

"Yes sir, we have a 7 minute head start to clear the blast radius Sir."

"Farewell 12" he mutters, then laughs dementedly.

56

CHAPTER 22

The best thing about training is the ability to think under pressure and not panic, so whilst Whiskey and I may have had a touch of Tourette's for a few minutes, we didn't start flapping, just fucking thinking, and he came up with the first suggestion.

"We need to go up. We need to go up. People always reinforce walls and doors, but hardly ever ceilings and floors. Get on my shoulders!"

So I did, and with the butt of my rifle I managed to knock a hole in the ceiling big enough to get my head and shoulders through. "It's fucking sealed mate! The room above us is sealed. Shutters here too. Fuck, fuckerty, fuck! I'm coming down" I said as I landed at his feet

"Right then. Through the wall we go then. What say you Mr Pro?"

He gave me a scowl and asked "how many rounds you got left?"

"7 in this clip and 3 full mags. You?"

"Same actually. Good boy for remembering to count them. Very professional" he added with a grin.

My response as usual, was to invite him to spin on my middle finger. "Right. Mind your ears Mr Pro. I'm about to discharge a projectile at said wall" I announced, before pulling the trigger 7 times, not even giving him enough time to plug his ears.

"Twat!"

"You're Welcome Mr Pro."

Whiskey attacked the bullet holes with the butt of his rifle and made a hole big enough to crawl through. We found ourselves in yet another sealed room. With a nice little 'surprise' contained within: C-4.

C-4 or Composition C-4 is a common variety of the plastic explosive family known as Composition C. C-4 is composed of explosives, plastic binder, and plasticizer to make it malleable, and usually a marker or odorizing taggant chemical.

It has a texture similar to modelling clay and can be moulded into any desired shape. C-4 is metastable and can be exploded only by the shock wave from a detonator or blasting cap. C-4 has a texture similar to modelling clay and can be moulded into any desired shape. Usually a dirty white to light brown colour it also has a distinct smell of motor oil.

When detonated, C-4 rapidly decomposes to release nitrogen, water and carbon oxides as well as other gases. The detonation proceeds at an explosive velocity of 8,092 m/s (26,550 ft/s).

Good news: there's no fire after all.

Bad news: there is NO chance of surviving the blast!

Urgent news: we need to get the fuck out of here, and quickly too!

Whiskey goes into full on Berserker mode now, kicking and gouging hole after hole through wall after wall until we reach what looks like the front door of this fucking place and try the handle, which is fucking locked. No problem for my remaining 3 rounds and an Adrenalin-powered kick though and we're finally out. Still well within the blast radius we start running full pelt across the gardens trying to put some ground between us and the C-4 display which we assume is imminent. We manage a reasonable distance

- Whiskey can shift when he needs to for a big fucker, and I'm like that bloke off the Virgin Broadband adverts that keeps doing the lightning strike thing - before there's a massive CRUMP!! As the whole world shifts on its axis and we both open our mouths and lay flat, hoping to be below much of the shockwave.

There are more CRUMPS and WHUMPS as we get up again and start running, looking for a vehicle of some sort to get the fuck out of here. Turns out we're in luck (sort of) as we come across a farm with a tractor in the courtyard and a pickup in the barn. Now I know what you're thinking: Hotwire the pickup, it's faster and safer than the tractor. Very true, but this isn't Hollywood. You can't Hotwire a 2017 vehicle in seconds without some serious technological hardware, but you can Hotwire a fucking old tractor in seconds. Especially one with the keys in the ignition. So while I start the tractor up Whiskey has kicked the farmers front door off its hinges and come out with the keys to the aforementioned pickup with a big fuck off smile on his face. "Race ya" he says as I decide that the tractor might not be such a good idea after all.

"Just testing Mr Pro. Seeing if you're switched on."

So while the ground and what I assume to be a network of underground tunnels collapses around us, we nail the pick up and make like the fastest cake in the world - scone. Get it? Scone - gone. Oh come on!

CHAPTER 23

C harles Addison, or Addy to a very select few, was what one might refer to as eccentric. He lived in a small town in Shropshire called Shrewsbury (which he pronounced Shrowesbury) and wore mustard-coloured corduroy trousers; a 'Ten Bob Millionaire' who 'worked in the city' and drank mild by the half pint, in the many local public houses, always keeping himself to himself.

He was a Civil Servant. A typical office-dweller in Human Resources for a Defence Logistics company. A snivelling worm-like man who loved the power being in HR gave him. He was able to lord it over anyone junior within the firm and did so with reckless abandon. Because of his secretive nature and his ability to lie and deceive all and sundry that everything was "fine. All on schedule. Running like clockwork" he had somehow found himself as a 'handler' for certain individuals within the businesses' sister company and had become somewhat of a Walter Mitty. He was seduced by the role with dreams of being a secret agent and swapping his usual half of mild for Martini's - shaken, not stirred -and a whole array of fantasies, some harmless, some not so. Like the high-end call girls he paid to act as his many 'conquests'. In short, he was far worse than the subordinates within the company he liked to look down upon and up to his eyeballs in debt to a Chinese 'gentleman' who he'd managed to pay off with a succession of credit cards before he started selling 'information'.

At first it had just been contracts for logistics and bid information for future workload, but if the Chinese gentleman had been shrewd and cunning, then his boss, the owner of Mencorp, had been a genius with his fingers in many pies.

Addy was playing a dangerous game. A very dangerous game.

CHAPTER 24

Menji was relaxing aboard one of his many ships, sipping a warm drink whilst his men and the ships' crew ran around feverishly sorting the cargo of kids out.

It had been an uneventful journey so far and he smiled as he remembered the mushroom cloud on the horizon as the C-4 detonated and set off a chain reaction of explosions. It had cleared evidence of any wrongdoing with the bonus of eradicating the two idiots who had put his operation at stake. He was ready for the 'Boy' but the soldier with him had been a surprise. He'd have to get his man on the ground in England to pay the blithering Mr Addison a visit for withholding information. He smiled as he imagined him soiling those awful mustard-coloured trousers whilst being 'interviewed' by his man.

"Fucking British!" He muttered "always so polite and well-mannered. Guòlái - come here!" He yelled at one of his bodyguards.

"I want the 'Brit' interviewed. He should know not to short change me. Arrange it!"

"Yes Sir. I shall call your man immediately."

Menji sat back and sighed - which the bodyguard correctly took as his cue to leave - and began thinking about what to do with his cargo of kids.

CHAPTER 25

We make our way across the country and up into the mountains with the fires of the once stately home still burning fiercely. Whiskey is driving whilst I think hard about a plan, any fucking plan really, but one that will get me back to England where I'm sure Menji is returning with those poor kids.

Whiskey had finished what he set out to do so it was up to me to finish what I had started. I needed to rescue those kids, fuck Menji up, and end his sick little operation, but not necessarily in that order.

Whiskey broke my silence "what you thinking then mate?"

"Just the enormity of what I've got to do" I replied.

"You? Surely you mean us? I'm a part of this now too pal. We've spilled blood together. We're brothers in arms now and we never leave a man, or boy in your case, behind. So what's the plan man?"

I laid out what I'd planned so far with nods of agreement and some suggestions. "But we need some transport. Something that floats or flies."

Whiskey grinned the biggest grin I'd seen from him so far as we turned onto a well-kept road into a small industrial estate in the middle of nowhere with a small plane and a helicopter both painted red and yellow. "Voila Señor 12. I present to you 'rescate de montaña' or mountain rescue to the layman. I pinged it on the way down and made a mental note. All we need now is somebody who can fly one of those things"

"Well Mr Pro, it just so happens that I can. Or at least my brain has been chipped or zipped to think I can."

"Let's give it a try then Señor 12"

Giving the plane a miss we make our way over to the helicopter and do the pre-flight checks quickly.

"Won't the plane be faster?" Whiskey asks.

"Probably, but we need a larger space to land it. The Helicopter will land almost anywhere solid and relatively flat. Plus, if that cunt Menji is going by boat you could take the controls while I jump out and kill him and his fucking Goons!" I reply whilst flicking buttons for the batteries, avionics and all the other gear that makes the magic happen. Then I cross my fingers as the blades start spinning and we get ready for take-off.

We set off, heading south in the hopes of finding a lorry capable of holding dozens of kids with or without shipping crates. Failing that, we'll follow the shipping route through 'Gib' and head back to the UK though without a watch or clock we don't actually know how much of a head start they have on us. It only feels like a couple of hours but Adrenalin, stress and anxiety distort time so if we can't find them on the road or the water they may well have flown.

I glance over at Whiskey "Sea or sky?"

"Definitely sea mate. It's easier to pass under the radar in a boat. Planes are monitored from the moment they set off, and where are they going to land?"

"Well, Menji has a runway at his own private fucking dockyard, so does that rule out a ship?"

"No mate. I still think sea. What would you do? It's a no-brainer for me. The runway would probably only be for local hops surely?"

I sit back again and weigh up the pro's and con's and come to the same conclusion so we press on, scouring the land and sea for something, anything that may point to a cargo of kids. What, I don't know, but we're not going to sit idle while those kids are in danger.

The hours fly by (pardon the pun) and we make our way inland to where I guess Menji's dockyard is, taking into account the time I was in the Police car for and the direction we took. "Yep! Bang on the money?" As we see the sprawling dockyard below us and make our way some distance past it to land and make our way back there on foot.

An hour later and we were back in the compound, hidden and waiting. "May as well keep stag if you wanna kip?" Suggested Whiskey. "I snatched a few when you were flying." "Ok then. Ta" I reply as I stretch out and relax thinking about how good it is to have someone alongside me. I'd been on my own for a long time. I thought I was happy in my own company, thought I enjoyed it; I realised now how wrong I'd been as I drifted into a much-needed sleep.

CHAPTER 26

It is dark now, with only a small fire to pierce the stygian blackness. Two men in Togas are approaching.

One is huge, muscled and covered in thick, dark hair. The other is thin and mean looking. Both hold spears and malicious grins.

I am on a cross and I struggle to break free as they approach, but the ropes around my wrists, ankles and waist bite deeper and scour my flesh, making me thrash and buck wildly.

They are talking low and menacingly in a language I intrinsically know to be Latin, with the odd audible phrase.

"Who is he?"

"What is he?"

"Not of this world!"

"Spill his blood!"

They close the distance to me and as they pierce my flesh they shape shift into Doctors wearing white lab coats and there is now a huge needle in my side in place of the spear as I hear one of the Doctors exclaim "it appears to have been successful!" and I scream silently into a huge sweaty palm.

"Shhhhh. It's ok 12. It's a dream. It's me, Whiskey. You ok mate?"

I open my eyes and get ready to explode for a second before I put a lid on it and focus on Whiskey.

I nod groggily as he removes his hand and points to the warehouse "they're here."

I sit up and take a second to get my bearings with the horrible thought that my dream was more than a dream. A flashback maybe? A memory, or memories distorted by my sleep-deprived brain. But now is not the time to dwell. Now is the time for action and I need to act, not think. Thinking leads to indecision. Indecision leads to hesitation. Hesitation leads to mistakes. Mistakes lead to death, and make no mistake about it, there will be death.

"Let's go" I mumble to Whiskey, and we make our way down to Warehouse number 8 and the ne'er do wells it holds.

CHAPTER 27

Watching through our respective scopes we spot Menji atop a shipping crate holding court with his many minions. "So we now hold them captive" he orders. "They have seen much. Too much to be released back into their Mule gangs. They could jeopardise this whole business. They are to be secured and under armed guard. I will personally see to it that your families know all about your failures should you fail. I play a background role normally, but this is far too important. Do we all understand!?"
There are nods of affirmation all around with a few "yes sirs!" Thrown in for good measure.

"Now" He continues, "we've successfully thwarted any plans to overrun us so far, but we mustn't become complacent or bask in the glory of our triumph. I have seen to it we are not disturbed here, but remain alert. Your lives 'literally' depend on it!"

He eyeballs each and every one of those present and steps down from his platform as we make ready our weapons and realise too late there's some fucker standing behind us pointing a gun at our backs and telling us to "turn a-fucking-round."

The average speed of a 12 year old boy is 16 mph in a sprint: covering 100 metres in 14 seconds, which means 10 metres in 1.4 seconds or 5 metres in .7 seconds. Add to that, the Adrenalin coursing through the veins of that same Boy triggered by fight, flight, or freeze and you can halve that again to .35 seconds.

So when the fucker stood 2 metres in front of us was disarmed and rendered unconscious in less than .1 seconds by yours truly it wasn't particularly impressive (or so I thought) to anyone. Except Whiskey, who raised his eyebrows and shook his head. "Fucking fast! Fucking unbelievable. Fucking Mini Bruce Lee."

"Come on then Sifu" I reply "we've got people to fuck up and kids to rescue."

After a cable tie and tape frenzy on 'Mr Unconscious' we move cautiously to the aforementioned shipping crate keeping to the shadows as silent as shadows; until Whiskey throws a fucking grenade in and body parts start sailing overhead.

"Thanks for the fucking warning!" I mutter as we close the distance and select single shot on our respective weapons.

Everything slows down now as we move fluidly through the kill zone like we're synchronised, slotting any fucker that appears and making our way to the door Menji disappeared through.

There are bodies everywhere and I shake my head before remembering what these bastards have done with the kids we're hopefully getting closer to rescuing. We move to either side of the door before opening it, Whiskey covering while I enter and clear the room the other side. The same room that has caged fucking baboons in and a massive bloke who looks like Bluto, complete with the beard and fucking undersized hat.

He launches himself at me with a punch that would have felled a mighty oak. I duck, roll to the side and reach for my knife... which isn't fucking there!

He comes again with a kick that catches me in the stomach and hurls me over a fucking baboon cage sending the primates within crazy.

I cover myself as he follows me over and rains punches into my forearms and biceps whilst my jellified, rattling brain thinks: Obviously angry, obviously fucking huge, but not particularly professional or switched on, so I pull his head in to my chest and throw my legs over his hips. He's too pumped to even notice as I grip his arm and pull him down to grab his wrist, then my own, pulling his arm up with his elbow pointing towards my face. I keep him controlled now and pull again whilst twisting and... pop! His arm, shoulder and wrist go. I release the useless limb as he rears up to cradle it with his good arm, and as he does I jab two fingers into his eyes. And a nice spear hand into his throat. He clambers backwards into the open arms of a crazed baboon reaching from its cage and I shut my ears to the horrific screeching and screams.

I turn to Whiskey "I think I've chipped my nail varnish mate" as I rub my now purple arms and smile.

He just shakes his head again and smiles "let's go Bruce".

We're moving again now. Together as a team. One covering, one firing. One breaching, one clearing and it's going relatively well until some fucker shoots me in the shoulder. Well more than just some fucker. It's a kid. About the same age as me and as he throws his gun aside and steams towards me like an Olympic sprinter I notice he's brought two mates with him. I open my mouth for a sarcastic comment when the little bastard fucking drop-kicks me in the chest.

Fucking WWE or what!? I try my best Mills Lane impression shouting "Let's get it on!" springing to my feet, pissed off and angry, turning to the three stooges who are now stood stock-still glaring at me while a voice I recognise booms through the many hidden speakers. "Well, well 'boy' seems I've underestimated you after all. You and your friend have done well to get here in one piece, though that won't be the case for much longer. I see you've met your successors 13, 14, and 15. They know all about you and as today is science day I've allowed them some practical work for a change. They're itching to dissect you and see what treasures you hold, so I shall leave you kids to it."

My new mates all immediately switch from passive aggressive to full on aggressive and I notice one seems to be the leader. A geeky looking twat with spectacles and an air of Harry Potter about him.

No wand or an owl but he does have a fucking huge lobotomy scar running around his head as do his two boyfriends.

"Expelliarmus" I shout as I run full pelt at 'Potter' and smash his fucking jaw in before realising his jaw isn't actually where I thought it was, and neither is he. I fucking hate Wizards!

CHAPTER 28

Whiskey stands in the shadows unnoticed as 12 goes berserk and starts screaming some Harry Potter nonsense, punching at thin air as one of the three 'kids' whips past him like something out of The Matrix.

He thinks for a second about Carrie-Anne Moss in that PVC cat suit - her arse like a couple of over-firm mini beach balls - before he spots one of 12's antagonists slinking past and grabs him, Mistaking him for just a kid instead of the jacked-up whatever he is and gets two palm slaps around his ears and a kick in the stomach that takes him off his feet.

"Little twat!" He roars whilst fending off the follow-up attack from his unbelievably savage and powerful assailant. Moving back with a speed belying a man of his size, Whiskey feints left before spinning around and hitting the 'kid' with a savage right hand which breaks his jaw but doesn't drop him. "Fucking fucker!" He mutters as he kicks his knee, pushing it to an impossible angle before launching himself back at the 'kid' and straddling his chest whilst trying to get to the little fucker's windpipe.

After what seems like minutes he finally gets the desired result as the little fucker's eyes close and he stops struggling. Whiskey climbs off him and reminds himself that it wasn't really a kid and actually a sick experiment though he can't help feeling guilty until an unearthly screech pulls him from his Adrenaline-induced deafness.

CHAPTER 29

Menji was angry. Very fucking angry, and again the common denominator was that little bastard and his buddy who had ruined his operation overseas, killed his personal guard, and somehow followed them back to England to do it all again.

He had watched the 12 year old 'thing' shoot, stab, and fight his way through his men to the now final hurdle like he was in some sort of far-fetched video fucking game. Still, he was about to be snuffed out once and for all by his three latest successes. Menji had overseen the programming and rebuilding of these three himself. They had been rebuilt using the finest software and hardware. Their pain receptors had been dialled down, their Adrenalin levels raised to impossible levels. Their bones had been reinforced with surgical grade Titanium by the best surgeons in the world; all on his payroll one way or another, and he had experimented with some top secret technology of his own, the same technology he would sell to the highest bidder, making his current vast fortune seem almost like a drop in the ocean. Ah... the ocean, the sea: back to where it all started. Where he had become the man he always knew he would be.

He thought of that night often. The night he had killed 12 men. The night he had escaped his pitiful existence on a huge boat he could no longer remember the name of. How he had killed the

'Boss' of the gang of thugs who terrorised the small fishing villages across his homeland. He had slit the man's throat and then proceeded to butcher him and wrap the parcels of meat in leaves, before leaving them as an unidentifiable food source for the villagers, almost as a parting gift.

He had washed himself clean, and found better clothing before he made his way to the docks to board the ship that would bring him closer to his goal of world dominance.

From there he had met an influential crime boss who was heavily into drugs and prostitution who became his mentor, before Menji realised he no longer needed mentoring and killed, butchered and served him up in a lavish meal for his family and closest allies.

The rest, as they say, is history.

CHAPTER 30

I had just spun around to locate 'Potter' when his fucking mate jumps in too! Now I've got two of the bastards trying to leather me!

I feel my adrenaline spike again and everything goes into slow motion as they converge on me with murder in their eyes. 'Potter' comes in from up high off a box he's just jumped on and his mate, who I haven't even thought of a fucking name for yet, comes in low, looking to take my midsection so I twist and fall like a ton of bricks as he blasts through the space where I was through a two way mirror and into another room giving me a few precious seconds to deal with 'Potter'. I grab his legs as he lands knowing he is too fast to keep trying to strike and roll on top of him. He throws some punches which I try to suffocate with my body trying to close the distance but they still fucking come sharp.

I eventually get the mount and rain down blows into his face and head while he tries to create space so he can, I suspect, 'shrimp' out but I'm not giving up my position easily so I hammer fist his nose, lips and eye sockets before plunging my thumbs into his eyes like a tub of fart putty and push till he stops that blood-curdling high-pitched scream... forever.

CHAPTER 31

The 'cargo' of caged kids are frightened. In fact, they're petrified. They can hear gunfire, explosions, shouting and that awful unworldly screech of what they correctly guess is somebody dying painfully.

They have been drugged, threatened, auctioned, beaten, and locked in cages like the ones they are back in now. The Chinese man and his friends have prodded, poked and inspected them all in the last 48 hours and they are close to hysteria as more noises come from the other side of a door which after much banging and hammering flies through the air and another kid walks through with ill intent on his face and what seems like a massive scar that encircles most of his head. He shouts, pounds his chest like King Kong and snatches a huge machine gun from the back of a truck before pointing it at a wall, pressing the trigger and watching as it booms and bucks, turning the wall to dust and brick fragments.

CHAPTER 32

The L7A2 General Purpose Machine Gun (GPMG or Gimpy) is a 7.62 x 51mm belt-fed general purpose machine gun which can be used as a light weapon or in a sustained fire role.

I ts rate of fire is up to 1000 rounds per minute with rounds flying at a velocity of 2,756 feet-per-second and a kill range of up to 1000 metres.
In short, it's an animal and a game changer so when 'Potter's' mate appeared amidst a cloud of cement dust and brick fragments from a hole in the wall my first thought wasn't "where did that hole come from?" It was something along the lines of "slap my arse and call me Susan. He's got a fucking Gimpy!"

He proceeded to do his best Arnie impression, holding the gun one handed and feeding the belt in with the other. The only thing he was missing was a big fat cigar. Oh, and about 10 stone of muscle. And the haircut. And the camo paint. And the big fucking knife. And the tactical vest. Oh, and the Predator alien thing. And the Red Indian bloke going on about "there's something out there waiting for us". Aaaaand, the little petite woman who he shouts "ged to de choppa!" to. So basically it was fuck all like Arnie actually. Probably not even the same fucking gun anyway.

Anyway. Where was I? Oh that's right, I was diving behind a huge steel stanchion which was part of the overhead crane, whilst watching Whiskey do the same thing, that and shitting myself, whilst thinking how I needed to work on my bulletproof training. And they say Males can't multitask.

I desperately needed to work my way around 'Dutch' (Arnie's character in the film for all you that didn't know) and take him down. The only problem is he has me pinned down and I can't move.

CHAPTER 33

Whiskey sees the same thing as 12 as the other 'kid' steps through the hole in the wall, firing the Gimpy one-handed. He ducks for cover, not because the 'kid' has seen him but because he doesn't fancy being shot anytime soon. Seeking cover behind an iron girder bolted upright he looks for a way to flank the 'kid' and relieve him of the fearsome General Purpose Machine Gun he's currently spraying the room with. He notices a tool box next to the workings of an overhead crane and sees hammers, sockets and spanners. He grabs a socket the size of a frag grenade - wishing it was - and gets ready to lob it at the 'kid's' head. He puts all his strength into it and launches it fearsomely scoring a direct hit on his head. Nothing. Not even a flinch. He does however start pouring fire at Whiskey's location which is only just wide enough to conceal his gargantuan frame. "Shit! Shit! Shit!" He mutters, scolding himself for the schoolboy error of getting himself pinned down. "I must be fucking tired or getting old. What to do old lad? What to bloody do?" He thinks out loud, laughing at his own language. "Bloody? Bloody? I sound like a Rupert, fresh out of Sandhurst!"

CHAPTER 34

I see my chance as 'Dutch' turns to concentrate his fire at Whiskey. I fling myself down the side of a conveyer belt and start crawling to flank him, thankful that I'm the size of an average 12 year old boy. Someone needs to get the Hoover and duster out behind here, I think, before realising I sound like my Mum. Shit! Where did that thought come from?

Anyway, back to the task at hand. I continue crawling till I estimate I'm ready to pop out behind 'Dutch' and spin his fucking head off his scrawny neck. I've just about had enough of that incessant boom, boom, boom now.

Craning my neck around some racking I spot him, still raining fire down on my Mucker with his back to me. I slip from cover and run full bore at him, jumping a few feet from his rear to land on his back wrapping that fucking ammunition belt around his pencil neck as the Gimpy slips from his hand. I twist and squeeze with my thighs around his midsection and fire half a dozen jabs into his temple knowing they lack the power to put his lights out. He responds by slamming his fists into the tops of my thighs and head butting me, aiming for my nose but getting my forehead as I tilt my chin down a nanosecond before impact. Still, it does the job and I lose my grip on him and hit the deck, before standing up and brushing myself off to meet his malevolent gaze.

"Let's do this" he squeaks in an almost comical voice before pulling a knife seemingly out of thin air and pointing it at me.

CHAPTER 35

K nives are fucking dangerous. They are silent, easily con-
cealed, require no reloading, cheap, and require little
skill to do big damage, so in spite of all the shit you see
on TV or YouTube it's not easy to disarm someone with a knife. In
fact, it's like trying to grab the rotor of a helicopter at full speed.
And that's just those that are unskilled with a knife so I knew I was
in trouble when 'Dutch' held his knife in an 'ice-pick' grip, got on
the balls of his feet and stalked me like the prey I was - fucking
Predator all over again!
I HAD to get that knife out of his hand before he shredded me like
a top secret document so I fell back on the Arnis I had been taught
(or maybe been programmed with!) many years ago.

As he came in with a figure of 8 slice/slash I stepped back knowing
the downward stab through the top of my collarbone would follow, then threw my left forearm at the right side of his head like I
was Superman on take-off before rolling his arm out whilst simultaneously grabbing his knife hand and kicking his kneecap as hard
as I could and snatching his blade away then dropping my weight
slightly and sticking the knife through the thick knotted muscle
of his upper leg. Lacking the strength now to pull the knife out,
I watched as he stumbled backwards into the path of Whiskey
who was in full swing with the biggest fucking spanner I had ever
seen. CLUNK! The spanner practically scalped him and he fell like
a felled tree at my feet where I stomped on his neck with all my re-

maining strength.

CHAPTER 36

Menji was livid! He'd watched once again on his network of cameras as the 'boy' and his companion had decimated his men and ruined his operation.

He needed to get away. He needed to escape, to live to fight another day. To regroup, rethink, re-establish and exact revenge on that 'boy' and all who stood in his way.

Never one to be caught out, Menji had built escape tunnels into all his properties, and as the sound of sirens filled the air and that pair of fucking soon-to- be-dead meddlers came into view he slipped away into the darkness of the aforementioned tunnels. Gone, but not forever.

CHAPTER 37

We had just emerged from the rear of a shipping container covered in blood, grime and gunpowder when a torch beam swept across our faces in tandem with a barked command "armed Police! Hands up and stay where you are!"

Whiskey and I stopped exactly where we were. Our weapons and kit had been dumped in the water and our clothes were barely recognisable anyway.

The torch beam stayed on our faces for a few seconds more before it switched off and the same voice asked "whiskey? Is that you? Fuck me, you look like shit! Come on, let's get you seen to."

Turns out the armed police was 'big Jim' who wasn't actually big at all. Just over 5 feet tall, with a face that had seen some action by the looks of it.

"Fuck me, big Jim! Am I glad to see you? What's going on?"

"Not sure yet mate. What you doing down here? Who's the kid? Are you ok son?"

"I'm ok I think" I replied. "Me and Dad were fishing. I know we shouldn't really be down here, but... Well, this is the best fishing spot. Please don't arrest us. We were just trying to get out. We've lost all our tack too. Dad!! Don't let them put us in jail!"

Big Jim looked a bit embarrassed and lowered his MP5 "oh. I didn't know you had a son Whiskey. Erm. Come on then. Get in the van and I'll er, get you through the gates. I can't be long though, the Guv is coming down in person for this one"

We headed for the Police van and jumped gratefully into the warm interior.

Whiskey leaned forward to talk to his mate: "er Jim. Any chance you could keep schtum about this? It wouldn't look too good for a PCSO to be caught breaking into a dockyard would it?"

"It's the least I can do mate" replied Jim turning to look at me. "You're Dad has saved my skin more than once lad. We've served all over the world together. He's a legend! Years we've known each other, and then he turns up at the nick wanting to be a Community Support Officer. Wasted if you ask me. With his skills he could be top of the tree. Still, I suppose you've had enough of that life eh ya big ugly bugger" he laughed.

"Come on, let's get you out of here. By the way, what's your name son?"

"Justin" I replied

"Well Justin. You're in safe hands there anyway.

How old are you Justin?" He asked whilst adjusting the rear view mirror to look at me.

I met his gaze in the mirror "I'm 12."

CHAPTER 38

Two days later I'd connected the dots.

I was still bruised and battered, sitting in the doorway of a shop in Addy's hometown, watching him leave The Lion Tap with a slight swagger on and a 'lady' on his arm.

They passed me by without a second glance and made their way down to the square. They were adjacent to the old music hall when I rang his phone. He seemed surprised as he pulled it out of his pocket and checked the screen: "hello?" He asked.

"It's me you traitorous old bastard! Ditch the prostitute and meet me down near the dingle. If I see you touch your phone again or do anything stupid you're fucking dead!"

I ended the call and watched him give his front door key to the girl and kiss her on the cheek.

5 minutes later and he was unsuccessfully trying to look calm and composed as I approached.

"Down by the river you twat!" I ordered.

"12. What's wrong?

"Just fucking move you silly old bastard before I knock that superior look of your face and dump you and that fucking stupid hat in the river. I mean, come on, who actually wears a fucking Fedora!?"

He was assessing now. Wondering what he could say or do to stall me. Wondering what I knew or how much of it.

"Well, I must say 12, this is somewhat clandestine. How are you? Are we safe to talk? This is not usual protocol old boy you know. Still, we are chums I suppose. So, what can I do for you?"

I tried to hide my anger as I replied through gritted teeth "you betrayed me. I've got questions. Lots of questions and for every wrong answer you give me I shall remove a piece of you and deliver it to your 'lady' friend who is sitting comfortably at 137 Percy Street as we speak."

He gulped in response and gabbled nonsensically "I, I can't answer. I don't know. I'm in trouble. The Chinese. They, they, they're all over me. Please. 12? Please. I'll tell you whatever you want to know, just...."

"Stop fucking blabbering!" I hissed. "I've got my questions first. It's me asking and you fucking answering ok?"

"Now. My memories. Are they real or something else?"

"Yes!" He blurted. "I mean no. I mean I don't fully understand myself. I mean, it seems impossible. But yes. I suppose it's beyond the realms of understanding but....."

"Calm the fuck down!" I snapped. "What do you mean? Yes, no, impossible? Make some fucking sense. Am I real or not?"

Now it was Addy's turn to look confused "of course you're bloody real. You're here aren't you? I mean, I'm definitely here and unless I'm talking to an empty cycle path then you're here too."

"No! I mean am I really centuries old? Or am I a normal 12 year old kid with a fucking hard drive where his brain should be?"

"No!" He shouted. But whether it was at me or the person who'd just shot him with a silenced Sig Sauer I didn't know, so I dived for him and dragged him into the water with me before any more rounds were forthcoming.

The cold water snatched my breath as I swam as hard as I could for the other riverbank and as I resurfaced behind a small fishing boat all was quiet. No gunman. No witnesses. And no Addy. Just that fucking stupid fedora floating downstream.

EPILOGUE

fortnight later Whiskey and I were sat in a cafe eating a full English.
"So what do you think?" He asked.

"I honestly don't know" I replied. "He said no. But was that to me or the mystery gunman? I mean, does he, or did he, actually know? I don't fucking know!"

"So we're still no further forward" he continued. "We don't actually know if he's dead. There's been no news of a body being found. There's not even been a missing person's report filed. But given his line of work I didn't expect there to be. So what you gonna do then 12?"

I sighed in response "keep searching. I need to know."

"Know what? The truth about you or whether Addy is really dead?"

"Both mate. Fucking both!

Printed in Great Britain
by Amazon

50198165R00054